Elsie
the Engineer
Fairy

By Daisy Meadows

ORCHARD

www.rainbowmagicbooks.co.uk

Jack Frost's Spell

Those brainy fairies make me cross.
One day Jack Frost will be their boss.
I'll solve each baffling mystery
And make each great discovery.

I'll steal their magic books away
And grow more crafty every day.
No clever-clogs in history
Will be as brilliant as me!

Contents

Chapter One
Straw Towers

"Good morning, Rachel," said Kirsty Tate.

Rachel Walker yawned, stretched and opened her eyes. For a moment, she couldn't think where she was. Then she remembered, and sat up in her sleeping bag feeling excited. She had spent the night at the Science Museum sleepover, and she had already shared three amazing adventures with her best friend Kirsty and the Discovery Fairies.

"Good morning," she said. "Is it time to get up?"

Kirsty nodded. All around them, children and grown-ups were yawning and crawling out of their sleeping bags. Mr Tate, who had come to the sleepover too, smiled at them.

"Let's go and find some breakfast," he said.

Still in their pyjamas, the girls rolled up their sleeping bags and followed Mr Tate to the far end of the Discover Space gallery. A table had been set up with bowls of cereal, fruit, toast and juice.

"Keep an eye out for Elsie the Engineer

Fairy," Kirsty said in a low voice. "Jack Frost still has her magical notebook. I hope we can help her before it's time for us to go home."

The night before, the girls had met the Discovery Fairies and heard about their troubles. Jack Frost had stolen their

precious magical notebooks. Without
the notebooks, no one in the human or
fairy worlds would be able to make new
discoveries. They had managed to find
three of the notebooks, but one was still
missing.

"We need to tell the museum staff
about the hidden gallery we found,"
Rachel remembered.

During their midnight adventure, the
girls had found a secret room full of
long-lost exhibits.

"Yes, but let's have some breakfast first,"
said Kirsty. "My tummy's rumbling."

As they were finishing their food, a
young man in museum uniform hurried
into the gallery.

"Good morning, everyone!" he said.
"I'm Ben, and I'll be your guide this

morning. I hope you slept well, and had a wonderful evening! Before you all go home, we have one last discovery for you. Please follow me."

Feeling excited, the group from the Discover Space gallery followed him through long corridors and up a flight of steps. At the top, they saw a big sign:

Explore Engineering Gallery

The children who had slept in the other galleries were already there.

"Come and join the fun!" said Ben, running up the steps ahead of them. "We've got a great challenge for you all this morning."

Rachel and Kirsty hurried up the steps and into the gallery. It was filled with light, and they gasped when they looked up. The ceiling was a high, domed roof made of glass. The early-morning sun was already shining brightly, and the sky was a brilliant blue.

"Welcome to the tallest gallery in the museum," said Ben.

He jumped on to a little podium and smiled at the crowd of people.

"This gallery celebrates some of the most amazing engineering works in the world," Ben said. "Engineers help us to make our dreams come true. They design incredible buildings and bridges so that we can go higher and further than ever before. Take a look around at some of the pictures and exhibits. You'll see some blueprints too. Blueprints are drawings that show how the buildings are put together. We hope you'll be inspired."

As he spoke, more museum staff came in, carrying large boxes.

"In these boxes you'll find pens, paper and straws," Ben went on. "In fact, you'll find everything you need to complete your next challenge. We want you to design and build a tower out of these straws – the tallest tower you can, right here in the gallery."

A gasp went around the room.

"How long have we got?" called a boy.

"It's an hour before the museum opens to the public," Ben said. "Whoever has the tallest tower when the doors open will be the winner. Ready, get set, go!"

Rachel squeezed Kirsty's hand.

"There are some pictures of the Eiffel Tower over here," she said, pulling her best friend over to the far wall. "Maybe we could get some ideas from that."

The gallery echoed with excited chatter and laughter. Everyone was rushing around to look at the exhibits.

"I've got a super tower design," someone said in a loud, boastful voice on the other side of the gallery. "Mine's going to be the best."

Chapter Two
Elsie Appears

Everyone got into groups and started
to build their towers. Rachel and Kirsty
began fitting their straws together.

"Oh no, my straw has torn," said
Rachel, disappointed.

"My tower won't stay up," a girl nearby
complained.

Soon, it was clear that everyone was having trouble with the challenge.

"No one has managed it," said Kirsty, gazing at the unhappy faces around her.

"Almost no one," said Rachel. "Listen."

From the other side of the gallery, the loud, boastful voice was still ringing out.

"My tower is awesome and amazing," the voice was saying.

"Shut up," squawked a second voice. "It's my tower, not yours."

There was a scuffling sound, and the girls exchanged a worried look.

"That sounded like a goblin squabble," said Kirsty.

"We'd better investigate," said Rachel.

They weaved through the groups of children, all trying to build towers. Ben and the other museum staff were helping,

but even they couldn't make the towers
work. They looked puzzled and upset.

"We have to find out if there are
goblins in here," said Kirsty. "If there
are, they must have the missing magical
notebook here. It would explain why
their tower is so good."

"And why everyone else is struggling,"

Rachel added. "Until Elsie has her notebook back, no engineering projects will work properly."

"Look over there," said Kirsty suddenly.

She pointed at a tall, sturdy tower of straws. It was standing next to the museum's model of the Empire State Building. Beside it, two boys were

pulling faces and jabbing each
other with their elbows. They were
wearing floppy nightcaps, bed socks
and green pyjamas.

"They're hiding their faces under those
nightcaps, but I'm sure they're goblins,"
Rachel whispered.

"Me too," said Rachel. "Look at their
enormous feet."

"There are only two of them," said Kirsty, looking around. "And I can't see Jack Frost anywhere. Let's go and talk to them. Maybe we can persuade them to do the right thing and give the notebook back."

The best friends held hands and felt a little braver. They walked up to the quarrelling goblins.

"Excuse me," said Rachel in a low voice. "We know who you are."

"And we think that you have something that doesn't belong to you," Kirsty added. "Elsie's magical notebook."

With a gasp, the taller goblin picked up a backpack and hugged it to his chest.

"Clear off," he snapped. "It's ours now."

"But if you keep it, you'll spoil things for engineers everywhere," said Rachel.

"Who cares!" said the shorter goblin, sticking out his tongue.

Kirsty took a deep breath and reminded herself to be patient.

"Without engineers to build them, there would be no bridges," she said. "There'd be no trains, no buildings, no machines, no motors."

"I like machines," the taller goblin admitted.

But the shorter goblin yanked on the sleeve of his pyjamas.

"Don't listen to them," he said. "They're friends with the silly fairies and you can't trust them. Come on."

Before the girls could say anything else, the goblins had skipped around the other side of their tower and disappeared into the crowd.

"Quickly, let's follow them," said Rachel.

Zigzagging among collapsing towers and grumbling groups, the girls raced across the gallery. They were just in time to see the goblins dive into a blue booth against the opposite wall. There was a sign above the door:

Engineering Film Experience

"Let's go in," said Kirsty. "At least if they're inside, they can't run away from us. We can try to change their minds."

Quickly, they slipped inside the little booth and shut the door. It was pitch black inside.

"Who's there?" said a quivering goblin voice.

Kirsty felt around on the wall beside the door.

"I can feel a light switch," she said.

She pressed it, but no lights came on. Then there was a little beep and a crackling sound.

"What was that?" squealed one of the goblins.

A large rectangle suddenly lit up on the wall.

"I think the film's coming on," said Rachel.

In the light from the screen, they could see five rows of seats. Rachel and Kirsty sat down at the front, and the goblins chose seats in the back row.

"Welcome to the Engineering Experience," boomed a voice from the screen. "Did you know that the chairs you are sitting on wouldn't be here without engineers? The floor under your feet and the roof over your head are there thanks to engineering wizards."

Pictures of amazing buildings and machines flashed across the screen. Rachel turned around and saw that the goblins were gaping at the screen.

"Ooh, I love films," the taller goblin sighed happily.

"Cinemas wouldn't exist without engineers either," said Kirsty in a loud voice.

"What's the matter with the screen?" asked the shorter goblin. "It's getting so bright."

29

"I can't see the picture," the taller goblin complained. "It's hurting my eyes. Where's the engineer?"

The middle of the screen grew brighter, and brighter, and brighter.

"I can see a shape," said Rachel. "Are those wings?"

"My heart's thumping faster," said Kirsty.

"Yuck," exclaimed the shorter goblin. "It looks exactly like a fairy."

"Hurray," cried Rachel, leaping out of her seat. "It's Elsie!"

Chapter Three
Jack Frost Interferes

The bright picture on the screen got clearer, and then Elsie the Engineer Fairy popped out of it, her glittering wheelchair hovering in midair. She was wearing a pink trouser suit and a white engineering helmet.

"Rachel and Kirsty, hello!" she called,

waving to them. "I'm so glad I found you."

"Us too," said Kirsty. "These goblins have got your magical notebook. We've been asking them to give it back."

The goblins pulled grumpy faces and folded their arms, but Elsie turned to them and gave them a beaming smile.

"Let me show you some of the amazing things that engineers have done," she said. "Maybe then you'll understand why I love engineering so much."

She waved her wand, and images flickered in the air around them. The International Space Station, the Great

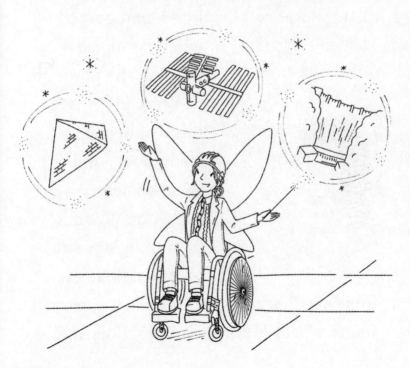

Pyramid and the Hoover Dam hovered above the chairs, and the Great Wall of China curved around the room.

"They look real enough to touch," said Rachel.

The taller goblin reached out his hand, and gasped when it rippled through the pyramid. "Look at this wonderful technology, and these ancient buildings. When human beings work together, there's no limit to what they can do. They can even make wheelchairs like mine," Elsie said, tapping it with a smile.

"Please give Elsie her notebook back," said Rachel gently. "Then she can help humans create new wonders of the world."

The goblin's eyes were like saucers.

"I think he might say yes," Kirsty whispered.

But then …
CRACK! There
was a flash of blue
lightning, and Jack
Frost appeared in
front of them. He
glared at Elsie,
Rachel and Kirsty,
and then stared in
amazement at the
pictures around him.

"You," he snapped, jabbing his finger at the goblins. "I've been waiting for you to bring me my notebook. I want to build an amazing tower in my garden."

"Hurray!" shouted the goblins. "We'll make the biggest, best tower ever!"

"But you're spoiling things for engineers everywhere," said Elsie, dismayed.

Jack Frost blew a raspberry at her, and the goblins squawked with laughter. Then there was another bright-blue flash of light, and Jack Frost and the goblins had gone.

"No!" Elsie cried out.

"Let's follow them," said Kirsty in an eager voice. "We know where they've gone. Maybe when we're there, we can find a way to get the notebook back."

"We have to try," Rachel agreed.

With a flick of Elsie's wand, all the incredible engineering pictures vanished from the air. They left behind a trace of golden sparkles, which started to swirl around into tiny ball shapes.

"They look like stars and planets in this dark room," Rachel whispered.

"It's like being in outer space," said Kirsty.

The girls smiled at each other, remembering their adventure with Aisha the Astronaut Fairy. More and more tiny golden sparkles landed on their heads, shoulders and arms. With a tickly,

magical shiver, their gossamer wings
unfurled. At the same time, they shrank to
fairy size.

"The golden sparkles look enormous
now," said Rachel.

"Big enough to carry us to Fairyland,"
said Elsie with a wink.

With another wave of her wand, silver
ropes appeared around the biggest,
roundest sparkle. They knotted themselves
to a wicker basket that hung under the
balloon.

Delighted, Rachel and Kirsty fluttered
into the basket. Elsie joined them, and the
balloon started to spin.

"Oh my goodness, it's like a fairground
ride in outer space!" cried Kirsty,
laughing.

The balloon twirled faster and the

fairies clung to each other, giggling. The magical sparkles grew brighter, until they were so dazzling that everyone closed their eyes. There was a sudden blast of cold air.

"Open your eyes," said Elsie. "We've arrived."

Chapter Four
An Unusual Team

When Rachel and Kirsty looked, they saw hills of gleaming white snow and sparkling ice. Jack Frost's Castle was ahead, grim and gloomy.

The shining balloon carried them around the castle and landed with a gentle bump in the garden. As they flew out of the basket, the balloon faded into the frosty air. With a swish of Elsie's wand, all three fairies were wrapped in fluffy coats.

"Look," said Rachel, pointing. "I think every single goblin must be outside."

There was a crowd of goblins squabbling in the middle of the garden. Around them were piles of wood and tools. Jack Frost was standing among them, holding a shining golden notebook.

"What are we going to do?" asked Elsie.

"Let's try helping them," said Kirsty suddenly. "Maybe if we show them kindness, they'll want to be kind to us."

"That makes sense," said Elsie, nodding.

Jack Frost thumped his fist on the notebook.

"What's the matter with you all?" he was

yelling. "The book's here, so start building my tower!"

"But how?" wailed a goblin.

"Have you tried working as a team?" said Elsie in her silvery voice.

All the goblins stopped chattering and turned to stare at her.

"Go away!" Jack Frost shouted. "Look at the sign!"

A rough wooden sign had been hammered into the snowy lawn:

"You should listen to what Elsie is trying to tell you," said Rachel.

"No fairy can teach me or my goblins anything," Jack Frost snapped.

"But you took the notebook because you wanted its magic," said Kirsty. "The magic of engineering. Elsie knows all about engineering."

Jack Frost thought for a moment, and then pointed at the wood and tools beside him.

"I want a tower," he said through gritted teeth. "But these nincompoops won't do the job."

"We've tried, boss," a goblin whimpered. "Every time we get to the first layer, the whole thing collapses."

"Why isn't this thing working?" Jack Frost demanded, waving the golden notebook at Elsie. "I've got the tools and the workers."

"Engineering is about more than tools and workers," said Elsie with a patient smile. "It needs imagination and a little spark of inspiration."

"That's why working as a team is so important for making discoveries," said Kirsty.

"Make it work!" Jack Frost demanded.

"I will help you," said Elsie. "Maybe then you'll see how much better it is to work together."

The fairies landed on the grass in front of the goblins, and Elsie held up her wand.

"The first thing that engineers make is a blueprint," she said. "That's a drawing that shows how everything is going to fit together and work."

"So, make one," growled Jack Frost.

"I need the magic of the notebook to help me," said Elsie.

Jack Frost held the notebook tightly, but allowed Elsie to rest her hand on it. She waved her wand, and a scroll of paper appeared in front of her. It unfolded by itself, and everyone saw that the shape of a tower was drawn on it.

"Now, I need everyone to think about what you want the tower to be," said Elsie.

"Easy to climb!" squawked one goblin.

"Tall," said Jack Frost. "Blue."

"And green," another goblin whispered.

The magical notebook glowed, and the drawing on the blueprint got more detailed.

"Now we have the blueprints, we need to make three teams," said Elsie. "Rachel, can you lead one team to organise the nails and equipment? Kirsty, please help the second team to cut the wood to the right size."

"What do you expect me to do?" Jack Frost barked.

He was frowning and still clutching the magical notebook.

49

"Jack Frost, you can help me to lead the third team," said Elsie. "We're going to follow the plans and start building."

The goblins were staring at Jack Frost, waiting for orders.

"Fine," he hissed. "Do what the silly fairy says."

Chapter Five
A Spell for Jack Frost

With a lot of pushing, shoving and grumbling, the goblins split into three groups. Rachel took the first group over to the messy piles of tools and nails.

"Come on," she said kindly. "Let's tidy up."

Kirsty found some measuring tapes and

showed her group how to measure the
wood to the right size.

"Keep checking the blueprint to see
how many pieces we need," she reminded
them.

Elsie showed her group how to start building the tower, and Jack Frost strode around them, checking their work.

Piece by piece, the tower grew higher. As each level was finished, Elsie tapped it with her wand to turn it frosty blue. Soon, the tower was as tall as the castle. A ladder reached all the way to a sturdy platform at the top. Most amazingly of all, there was

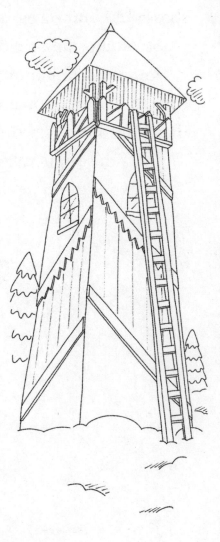

no squabbling. The goblins worked peacefully side by side.

Finally, a goblin tapped the last nail in place and slid down the ladder.

"My tower," cried Jack Frost in delight. "Oh, I'm so marvellously clever and talented. I am a genius!"

"I think that everyone on the team should feel proud," said Kirsty.

"Especially Elsie," said Rachel. "Don't you think that she deserves a thank you for all the help she gave you?"

Jack Frost shrugged and carried on grinning up at his blue tower.

"I'll call it the Jack Frost Tower," he said. "JFT for short."

"Elsie helped you," said Kirsty. "It's fair that you should do something for her."

"I never promised to be fair," Jack Frost said with a snarl. "Why should I? I've got what I wanted, and that's all I care about. All of Fairyland will be talking about my amazing tower."

Suddenly, Rachel had an idea.

"Oh no they won't," she said in a loud voice.

Jack Frost turned to glare at her.

"What do you mean?" he yelled. "Of course they will."

"How can they?" Rachel went on. "No one knows it's here. The only way to get everyone talking about the tower is to invite them all to see it."

Kirsty exchanged an excited glance with her best friend. She had guessed what Rachel was thinking.

"What are you talking about?" Jack Frost asked.

"In the human world, when there's a new building, they have a special ceremony," said Kirsty. "Lots of guests are invited. There is yummy food and drink, and a big ribbon gets tied across the new building."

"Yes, and someone very important cuts the ribbon and says 'I declare this building open'," Rachel added.

Jack Frost's eyes had opened very wide.
The goblins started licking their lips and
talking about food.

"Can we have green slime cakes?" one
of them pleaded.

"Marshmallow burgers?"

"Pondweed pies?"

"Sticky bog-toffee?"

"Fizzy mould-berry juice?"

"And an enormous blue ribbon," said
Jack Frost, rubbing his hands together.
"Yes. Invite everyone!"

"It's going to be difficult for Elsie
to send invitations to everyone in
Fairyland," said Kirsty. "Without her
notebook, her magic might not be strong
enough."

"But I want everyone to be talking
about my tower," Jack Frost grumbled.

Rachel and Kirsty held their breath
and crossed their fingers. Jack Frost
narrowed his eyes as if he were thinking
hard. Then he took the golden notebook
from under his cloak and shoved it on to
Elsie's lap.

"Take it, then," he said. "But you'd
better make sure that everyone in
Fairyland is here to see my tower."

The notebook glowed brightly as Elsie picked it up and hugged it. She raised her wand and whispered a spell.

"Discovery magic, be my guide.
Send this message far and wide:
Come to Jack Frost's tower today
To eat and drink, and laugh and play.

We built a tower with a view,
To make Jack Frost's big dream come true.
Now come and celebrate with me
The opening of JFT!"

Chapter Six
Opening Ceremony

A swarm of blue envelopes streamed out of the tip of Elsie's wand. They flew into the air and spread out in all directions.

"They will cover all of Fairyland in the twinkling of a star," said Elsie.

"But what about the snacks?" the goblins wailed.

Elsie waved her wand again, and long tables appeared around the bottom of the tower. Half the tables were laden with goblin treats. The other half had bowls of strawberries, raspberries and blueberries, lemon-puff pies, fairy cakes, triangle

sandwiches and so many other delicious
dishes that Rachel and Kirsty couldn't
count them all. Between the tables were
fountains of frothy hot chocolate.

"There's just one thing missing," said
Elsie. She tapped her wand against one
side of the tower. A wide blue satin

ribbon tied itself around the tower with a huge bow. Jack Frost smiled.

Just then, the air filled with music. Everyone looked up, and saw fairies flying towards them from all directions. They were waving and smiling. A shining white carriage, pulled by a rainbow-coloured unicorn, landed softly in the snowy garden.

"It's the king and queen," said Rachel.

The door opened, and out stepped Queen Titania and King Oberon. Fairies landed all around them, curtseying.

"Manners!" Jack Frost hissed at the goblins.

They all bowed so deeply that their noses got buried in the snow.

"Welcome to my opening ceremony," said Jack Frost in a proud voice. "As you

can see, this is the best thing that has ever
been created in the history of Fairyland.
Clap!"

The fairies clapped politely. Then Jack
Frost pulled a large pair of silver scissors
from inside his cloak.

"Look at the handles," Kirsty whispered

to Rachel with a giggle.

The scissor handles were carved into the shape of goblins, one sticking his tongue out, and the other pulling a face.

Jack Frost marched up to the ribbon.

"I now declare Jack Frost's Tower officially open," he said in his loudest voice. "Make sure you all talk about it lots, and remind each other how clever I was to build it."

He cut the ribbon, and everyone cheered. Then the goblins rushed for the food. Elsie wheeled her chair over to Rachel and Kirsty.

"This is a happier ending than I could have ever imagined," she said. "I thought that Jack Frost was going to keep my magical notebook for ever. Instead, he gave it back and has even thrown a party!"

"This is definitely a day to remember," Rachel agreed, laughing.

"It's thanks to you two," said Elsie. "I would never have managed this without your help. Thank you."

The other Discovery Fairies came fluttering up to them and they all shared a big hug.

"Thank you for everything," said Aisha. "Because of you, Mission Control can work properly again."

"And exciting discoveries will still be made every day," Annie added.

"We'll never forget what you have done for us," said Orla.

"And we'll never forget our adventures with all of you," Kirsty replied. "It has been the busiest sleepover ever."

Elsie laughed, and blew each of them a kiss.

"Talking of the sleepover, it's time I sent you back," she said. "I hope we'll see you again soon."

Rachel and Kirsty waved to their fairy

friends, and then everything went dark.

"Where are we?" Rachel asked.

"I think I know," said Kirsty. "We've come back at exactly the moment we left. That means we must still be inside the little cinema booth."

"My wings have disappeared," said Rachel. "I guess we're human again too."

Holding hands, the girls felt their way past the cinema seats. They found the door and slowly pushed it open. The Explore Engineering gallery was bustling with people. Tall towers of straws swayed upwards towards the glass ceiling. Happy laughter and excited chatter filled the air.

"Everything is back to normal," said Kirsty with a sigh of relief.

"Are you disappointed that we don't have a tower of straws?" Rachel asked.

Kirsty laughed.

"We've just built a wooden tower in Fairyland with the help of Jack Frost, Elsie the Engineering Fairy and goodness knows how many goblins," she said. "I feel as if we've already won!"

"Let's go and tell Ben about the secret gallery we found last night," Rachel said.

Walking carefully around the delicate towers, the girls found Ben chatting to Mr Tate. Quickly, they explained about the hidden exhibits down in the basement, and the clever lock that they had found. Ben was very excited.

"It sounds as if you have solved a very old mystery indeed," he said. "I can't wait to see it. What an amazing discovery!"

Mr Tate hugged them proudly.

"I had no idea that sleepovers could

be so exciting," he said. "Well, such an important discovery deserves an important reward. What would you like to do next?"

Rachel and Kirsty shared a look.

"I think what we'd both like to do most of all is to go home," said Kirsty, smiling. "I want to write everything down in my notebook."

Rachel grinned. "And then we'll be ready for some more discovering. Discovering new things is the best feeling in the world!"

The End

Now it's time for Kirsty and
Rachel to help ...

Ivy the Worry Fairy

Read on for a sneak peek ...

"I can't believe we're both here," said
Rachel Walker.

"Me neither," said her best friend, Kirsty
Tate. "It was the best surprise ever when
we arrived last night and saw you."

It was Saturday morning, and the
girls were looking forward to a relaxing
weekend at the Olive House Family
Mindfulness Retreat.

"Our parents are pretty good at
keeping secrets," said Rachel, laughing.
"They planned for us to be here together,
and they didn't say a word about it."

The girls shared a very special secret of

their own. Ever since they had first met,
they had been friends with the fairies.
They had been to Fairyland many times,
and were always ready to help the fairies
foil bad-tempered Jack Frost and his
naughty goblins.

"We even get to share a bedroom," said
Kirsty.

She sat on her bed and bounced up
and down. The room was pretty, with
sunshine-yellow curtains and a vase
of daffodils on the dressing table. The
window looked out over the big garden
of Olive House.

There was a knock on the door, and
Rachel's mum came in with Kirsty's
mum.

"Your dads have gone for an early
walk and we're going to join the

morning meditation class," said Mrs
Walker. "Would you like to come?"

"Yes please," said Kirsty, jumping to
her feet. "I want to try everything this
weekend."

"Me too," said Rachel. "Josh made
meditation sound amazing."

Josh was the Mindfulness Guide at
Olive House. The girls had met him
when they arrived the evening before.

"I thought so too," said Mrs Tate. "I
hope I can be as calm and relaxed as
Josh by the end of this weekend."

The meditation class was being held in
the summerhouse in the garden. It was
a sunny morning and birds were singing
loudly in the leafy trees. When Rachel
and Kirsty reached the summerhouse,
they stopped in surprise. Josh was there,

but he didn't look calm. His forehead was wrinkled with worry lines.

"Good morning, Josh," said Mrs Walker.

"I'm afraid it's not a very good morning so far," said Josh.

Read **Ivy the Worry Fairy** to find out what adventures are in store for Kirsty and Rachel!

Calling all parents, carers and teachers!
The Rainbow Magic fairies are here to help
your child enter the magical world of reading.
Whatever reading stage they are at, there's
a Rainbow Magic book for everyone!
Here is Lydia the Reading Fairy's guide to
supporting your child's journey at all levels.

Starting Out

Our Rainbow Magic Beginner Readers are perfect for first-time readers who are just beginning to develop reading skills and confidence. Approved by teachers, they contain a full range of educational levelling, as well as lively full-colour illustrations.

1

Developing Readers

Rainbow Magic Early Readers contain longer stories and wider vocabulary for building stamina and growing confidence. These are adaptations of our most popular Rainbow Magic stories, specially developed for younger readers in conjunction with an Early Years reading consultant, with full-colour illustrations.

2

Going Solo

The Rainbow Magic chapter books - a mixture of series and one-off specials - contain accessible writing to encourage your child to venture into reading independently. These highly collectible and much-loved magical stories inspire a love of reading to last a lifetime.

3

www.rainbowmagicbooks.co.uk

"Rainbow Magic got my daughter reading chapter books. Great sparkly covers, cute fairies and traditional stories full of magic that she found impossible to put down" - Mother of Edie (6 years)

"Florence LOVES the Rainbow Magic books. She really enjoys reading now" - Mother of Florence (6 years)

The Rainbow Magic Reading Challenge

Well done, fairy friend – you have completed the book!
This book was worth 5 points.

See how far you have climbed on the
Reading Rainbow opposite.

The more books you read, the more points you will get,
and the closer you will be to becoming a Fairy Princess!

How to get your Reading Rainbow
1. Cut out the coin below
2. Go to the Rainbow Magic website
3. Download and print out your poster
4. Add your coin and climb up the Reading Rainbow!

There's all this and lots more at
www.rainbowmagicbooks.co.uk

You'll find activities, competitions, stories, a special
newsletter and complete profiles of all the
Rainbow Magic fairies. Find a fairy with your name!